THE GIANT'S BOOT

Ritchie felt himself lifted into the air.

THE GIANT'S BOOT

Written by
CHARLES ASHTON

Illustrated by
PETER MELNYCZUK

WALKER BOOKS
AND SUBSIDIARIES
LONDON • BOSTON • SYDNEY

For Robin

First published 1995 by Walker Books Ltd
87 Vauxhall Walk, London SE11 5HJ

2 4 6 8 10 9 7 5 3 1

Text © 1995 Charles Ashton
Illustrations © 1995 Peter Melnyczuk

This book has been typeset in Plantin Light.

Printed in England

British Library Cataloguing in Publication Data
A catalogue record for this book is available from the
British Library.

ISBN 0-7445-4106-9 (Hbk)
ISBN 0-7445-4333-9 (Pbk)

CONTENTS

CHAPTER ONE
7

CHAPTER TWO
19

CHAPTER THREE
31

CHAPTER FOUR
39

CHAPTER FIVE
53

CHAPTER SIX
67

CHAPTER SEVEN
81

CHAPTER EIGHT
93

*Thousands of years before Ritchie was born,
a giant had lost its boot.*

Chapter 1

Thousands of years before Ritchie was born, a giant that lived on the hill nearby had lost its boot. The giant had gone stumping and banging about for a while, searching for the boot; but in the end, when it couldn't find it, it had done what most giants do when they're stuck: lain down and gone to sleep.

The lost boot had fallen into the river, and as it got thoroughly soaked it began to shrink. Time passed and the boot went on getting smaller and harder, until in the end it was no bigger than an ordinary human boot – but it was made of stone.

Meanwhile the river got smaller too, until it was no more than the grey stream that wound, soft and fat, through Ritchie's village, from the hill at one end out through the thick-wooded Den at the other, where many of the village children played.

It was Ritchie who found the stone boot lying there in the bed of the stream. It happened one summer when the water was quite low and he and his friends were building a dam under the arching trees. Ritchie splashed along towards the odd, L-shaped stone, thinking it might be useful for the dam. He bent and heaved at one end of it but couldn't budge it. He was about to leave it, but thought he'd take a last heave at the other end, which didn't look quite so heavy. His fingers easily found a grip; but then something made him stop and look closer. The stone seemed hollow, and water was swilling in and out of an oval-shaped opening with a soft *sloop-gloop*. That was when he realized what the stone was. And then he noticed marks in it like stitching – tiny, delicate stone stitches.

He left the stone boot lying where it was. He was quite delighted with his find but didn't want to tell his friends about it just yet, not until he'd had a good look at it himself.

However, it was a long time – more than a year – before he got a chance to do this. That same evening after he had found the boot the rain started: days of heavy rain which swelled the stream to the top of its banks. Even when the water did go back a little, Ritchie could see no more than the top of the boot rippling the surface. His one attempt at getting hold of it was a complete disaster: he lost his footing and fell in the water, hitting his head on the stone. He slodged home leaving a trail of puddles all through the village and was promptly forbidden to go down to the Den alone again because he could have killed himself.

He told his older sister, Maisie, what he had been trying to do. She was interested, but didn't want to help him. "There's Ritchie's stone boot," she told her friends every time they went past that part of the stream and saw the smooth black shape lodged out in the current. Ritchie didn't mind too much about her not keeping his secret, because Maisie's friends thought it was just one of his make-believes.

So winter and the dark nights came. Ritchie stayed indoors at Hallowe'en because of the ghosts that Dad said went about on that night. Then the weather got colder, and Ritchie watched the fire-ghosts

Ritchie lost his footing and fell in the water.

chasing each other up the chimney. And then the snow came and he saw the snow-ghosts flashing up in the bright air. And at last the spring came again, and all the ghosts turned themselves into birds which woke him up early in the grey mornings.

In April there were warm days and a whole month without rain. People said it was the unusually warm spring which caused the landslip on the hill. Hundreds of people went up to look. Dad took Maisie and Ritchie one weekend. On the far side of the hill from the village a whole section of the hill had simply collapsed away, leaving a wall of rock where there had once been smooth green grass. The rock didn't look the way cliffs normally look: no moss or grey lichen, no little angles where weeds or small trees grew: just sharp-edged brown stone that seemed to huddle back from the light of day.

The dry weather may or may not have caused the landslip, but it was certainly the dry weather which made the level of the stream drop so quickly. Ritchie, who had not been to the Den now for some while, was allowed to go by himself again after he had promised not to do anything stupid. But he needn't have bothered, for the stone boot was gone.

It had not simply disappeared: it had been dragged off. Ritchie didn't notice this to begin with, but when he took Maisie along and showed her, she said, "Look, there's a groove in the ground where it's been dragged."

The groove ran up the soft bank of the stream, over the little path, through a patch of furry-leaved comfrey, through a bed of dead leaves, over the grass beside the broad main path – and disappeared. "End of groove," said Maisie.

"No boot," said Ritchie.

The loss spoiled the summer for him. It wasn't that it was a bad summer: it was just that he had wanted the stone boot; and if he couldn't have it, at least he wanted to know what had happened to it. He did ask Dad about it, but Dad looked blank. "I didn't even know there were stone boots," he said, "so how would I know what happens to them when they disappear?"

There was worse to come. Mum got ill, and no one seemed to know what was wrong with her. She went into hospital three times, but she never seemed any better when she came home. As the summer came to an end she took to her bed and spent more and more of her time there. Days came when she was only getting up in the morning to get everyone's breakfast and then going back to bed. She would get up at suppertime, but would be back in bed again long before Maisie and Ritchie were. It meant Dad had to do more and more about the house, clearing up and cooking the meals.

Mum looked all right. Maisie said there was no blood, so there couldn't be anything really wrong with her. She looked cross a lot of the time, and she looked pale a lot of the time, and she didn't wash her hair enough and she didn't seem to want to talk to anyone.

The summer came to an end, and Maisie and Ritchie went back to school and Dad went back to work. Dad was a teacher, though not at Maisie and Ritchie's school. When he came back one night, just before going off to make the supper, he flopped down in a chair and said, "I hate kids."

"We're kids," said Maisie. "Does that

mean you hate us?"

"No, I don't hate you, I love you," Dad replied tiredly. "So that means you're not kids."

"What are we then?" said Maisie.

Dad drew Maisie and Ritchie over and lifted them so that one was sitting on each of his knees. "You," he said, "are the treasures of my kingdom, the prop of my age, the blessing of my hoar head, and the apples of my two eyes. Do you want anything else?"

"No," said Maisie. "That's enough. That's good."

Ritchie did not think about ghosts that Hallowe'en. Nor did he see any ghosts, either in the flames of the fire or in the snow that came early, in the second week of November. The ghosts were all in his head, where he couldn't see them: the ghost of a stone boot, the ghost of Mum as she used to be, big and busy and laughing and in charge of everything.

Ritchie put his hand inside the boot.

CHAPTER 2

"Toast's burning, Dad!" Maisie called. Mum had taken to her bed altogether, and Dad had to get them all ready in the morning.

"Damn," said Dad, running through to the kitchen. "Quick, out of my way Maisie – it's in flames."

Maisie ducked out of his way, which was not easy because the kitchen was very narrow. It had been all right when Mum was in charge of it, because she had had things organized so that no one ever had to pass.

Black toast, black smoke, red flames and all, Dad threw it out of the window onto the snow, where it hissed for a second and then went dead. "Four black squares," Maisie remarked. Dad yanked the window shut, and as he did so his arm brushed against a little glass bottle on the sill, sending it smashing into a thousand pieces in the sink.

"Damn," said Dad, as he put some more toast on. "No one put their hands in the sink. Maisie, will you watch the toast this time."

"But I've got to eat my cereal, Dad – you said."

"Oh, all right." Dad went back to helping Ritchie with the cuffs of his school shirt, whose buttonholes were so tight that no one (except Mum) could ever get the buttons done up.

The second lot of toast burned.

"Eight black squares," said Maisie.

The third lot of toast was just warm, and

quite soft. "Think of it as fresh-baked bread," said Dad.

"I like toast for breakfast," said Ritchie.

"How's your shirt come out of your trousers already?" said Dad. "Stand up, I'll tuck it in."

Quarter to nine. They were too late to walk to school. Dad said he would take them in the car. "You look like a monkey," Maisie told Dad as they went out into the snow. "All hairy."

"Oh, my God, I've forgotten to shave," said Dad. He looked at his watch. "Oh damn, damn – I'll never make it to school in time. All right – I'll just say I'm growing a beard. I'll just have to grow a beard."

"Giants have beards," said Ritchie.

"John Anderson's dad has a beard," said Maisie, and John says all his food gets caught in it – potatoes and cream, and jam and spaghetti sauce -"

"Get into the car," Dad ordered.

"Oh, look at the time, look at the time," he kept saying as he got the car started and backed it out onto the road.

"Mum just never gets up," Maisie said. "She is just *so* lazy."

"She's not lazy," Dad snapped. "She's ill."

"Poor Dad has to do everything." Maisie sighed.

There was a crunch. "You've hit the wall, Dad," Ritchie announced.

"The wheel spun in the snow," Dad snarled.

They were late for school. Ritchie's shirt was hanging out again, and one of his cuff buttons had come undone and he had butter down his tie. Maisie pointed all this out to Dad as they got out of the car. "Tough," he said, and screeched off down the road to the next town, where his school was.

Over the weeks that followed Dad got better at managing the toast, and there were some days when they got to school on time, but no one could work out how to make Ritchie's shirt stay tucked into his trousers. It was always a great relief when the weekends came and the day could get going in a sloppier and more pleasant fashion. Dad let Maisie and Ritchie watch television while he had a long lie in bed. Mum never got up at all now, and there were days when Ritchie even forgot she was in the house.

The heavy November snow didn't go away, because it remained unusually cold. Week followed week, and fields and rooftops and gardens remained white and muffled. Children did so much sledging that days came when they couldn't be bothered doing any more. Snowploughs came and cleared the roads, but no one could see where the paths were, and gradually new paths came to be made over the snow, going through places, across fields, across the frozen stream, where no one normally went.

One Saturday afternoon Ritchie was walking on his own along one of these new paths. You got on to it from the edge of the village green if you squeezed through a thin part of a hedge. It crossed a piece of sloping ground between the stream and a row of houses. Ritchie didn't know if he was supposed to be walking there. He had a feeling that he might be going through the gardens of the houses, but he could see no fences to show where the gardens might be. The air was blue-grey, quite bright, but misty, so the snow was not as dazzling as it was on some days.

He stopped. This was definitely a garden.

He knew this because it was full of garden gnomes and other stone ornaments: wheels, model houses, statues – a boy holding a ball, a girl with no clothes on carrying a pot – each with its own thick cap of snow. It was a garden of statues. He peered here and there, undecided whether to go on or turn back. He couldn't help feeling interested.

All at once he ran forwards, right into the middle of the snowy garden. There, perched halfway up a silly broken-off ladder, he saw the stone boot.

There was no mistaking it, even though the top and the toe were swathed in snow. It was the same size, the same shape, the same dark colour, with the same minute stitching. He put his hand on it. Even though it was over a year since he had touched it and it had been cool and wet then and was dry and freezing now, it still felt the same. It was his stone boot. Whoever lived here had waited till the level of the stream had fallen that April and had hauled it out and brought it here. Probably one of Maisie's friends had been giggling about it and some grown-ups had been listening and had believed her. That made Ritchie cross. It didn't seem fair, when he had found it. It would be quite fair if he took it away now.

Carefully, Ritchie removed the snow that covered the top of the boot. It sat like a plug over the hollow part and had not fallen inside. The space inside was quite small and the sides of the boot were quite thick. It would be very heavy. Ritchie realized he wouldn't be able to carry it off by himself, even if that was what he decided to do.

He put his hand inside the boot. His arm was just long enough to get to the bottom.

Suddenly   something   very   strange

26

happened. Although, in a way, he knew he was still standing there in the snow, it seemed to him that he himself was actually inside the boot, only the boot was no longer a boot but a rocky tunnel leading straight into a hillside. And he was walking down this long, straight tunnel, and when he got to the end of it of course he had to turn a corner. And just round the corner he came up against two huge things, one pale, one dark, towering above his head, like great wide slabs. He peered at them intently. One – the dark one – was slightly taller and slightly broader than the other, and had a rounded top. The top of the pale one was a series of knobbles of different sizes.

Next moment he had come back to himself and was standing in the snow again, pulling his arm out of the stone boot. But he realized what he had been looking at, in

*Round the corner, Ritchie came up against
two huge things.*

there, in the dark tunnel in the rocks: feet –
two feet, feet of someone lying on his back,
one bare foot and one with a shoe on. But
huge feet, impossibly huge. A giant's feet.
A giant lying under a hill, with one shoe on.
Or perhaps not a shoe: perhaps a boot.

Ritchie turned away and started walking
thoughtfully back the way he had come.

The air became bluer. Evening was
coming on. A pale half-moon glimmered
faintly in the darkening sky.

The man was waving angrily at Ritchie.

CHAPTER 3

There was a small black bobbing thing in the snow when Ritchie got back home. It was Can't-Wait, their three-legged black and white cat. Can't-Wait had been run over two years before by the local gamekeeper, who didn't like cats. The vet had saved his life, but not his front leg. Can't-Wait managed very well on three legs, though he had a queer sort of hobbling run and just now his chin kept scooping out little grooves in the snow as he came towards Ritchie.

As it was the weekend, Dad had had all afternoon to get the supper ready, so he was quite calm for most of the evening, with only a small upset at bedtime, due to Can't-Wait's over-friendliness. "I want 'Jack and the Beanstalk'," Ritchie said when Dad had settled down again.

"What, again?" said Dad. "You're always asking for that."

At the end of the story, Ritchie said, "Do giants wear boots or do they have bare feet?"

"Boots, I should say," said Dad.

"Bare feet," said Maisie.

"If they wore boots, what would the boots be made of?" Ritchie asked.

"I don't know," said Dad. "Leather, I suppose, same as any boots."

"They're not made of anything," Maisie said. "Giants have bare feet."

"Would the boots shrink if they got into water?" Ritchie asked.

"I suppose so," said Dad.

"No, they wouldn't," Maisie put in.

"Would they shrink into stone?"

"Only if they petrified," Dad replied.

"Can't-Wait was petrified when Dad tried to grab him," Maisie said.

"Not that kind of petrified," said Dad. "Petrified means turned into stone. It sometimes happens to things, but it takes thousands and millions of years."

"I saw a giant's feet," said Ritchie, "with only one boot on."

"Ritchie's always seeing things," Maisie remarked. "He sees ghosts chasing each other up the chimney."

"I don't," said Ritchie, who had forgotten all about the fire-ghosts of last year.

"Time to go to sleep," said Dad, heading off an argument.

Ritchie dreamed of the giant. The giant was sleeping, and it seemed that it was sleeping because it had lost its boot.

* * *

Monday came, and school again. Monday mornings were quite well organized, because Dad would get things ready on Sunday night. Dad got a letter through the post. "The district nurse will be coming regularly," he announced, "to see Mum."

"Why?" asked Ritchie.

"Because she's ill," Dad said. "She needs to be looked after."

Ritchie hardly ever saw Mum now. It was better just to forget she was there.

"Mum *seems* to be ill," said Maisie. "But it could just be that she's lazy."

"Go and get your shoes on," said Dad.

After school, Ritchie could stand it no longer. He had to go and see the stone boot again. He was supposed to go home with Maisie, but he told her he was going home with some of his friends and then slipped off in the opposite direction, towards the Den-end of the village. He lurked for a while at the bridge, then crossed the village green – or the village white, as many of them called it now – and joined the snow-path he had found the day before between the stream and the row of houses. Before long he was standing gazing at the stone boot halfway up its stupid stone ladder.

It was there. That was it. It was his boot.

Ritchie was in full view of the windows of the houses, but he was so intent on the boot he forgot all about being easy to see. He went forward, took hold of the boot in his arms and lifted it off the rung of the ladder where it was balanced.

It was far too heavy. For a couple of seconds he staggered backwards and forwards as it steadily slipped from his grasp. In the end he let go and jumped back to save getting his toe squashed. The heel of the boot hit the snow and then the whole thing toppled over.

But as soon as it hit the ground something started happening: a difference in the air, a difference in the ground. Everything was trembling. The ground was actually shaking, and the powdery surface of the snow was stirred about like icing sugar shaken into a bowl. And quite distinct but very distant, perhaps from the hill at the other end of the village or perhaps from beyond it, there came a shout: "Hoy!" And echoes seemed to rustle among the treetops and chatter along the frozen surface of the stream: "Hoy-hoy-hoy-hoy-hoy..."

And then very distinct and very near there came another shout. "Hoy! What do you think you're doing?" And there was no doubt where this shout was coming from, because Ritchie could see the man who had shouted. The man was standing at the door of one of the houses – not the one the statue-garden belonged to but the one next to it – and was waving angrily at him.

Before he had time to think properly that he was in considerable trouble, Ritchie got a chance of escape. An avalanche of snow, possibly loosened by the trembling of the ground, slipped from the roof right down on top of the man at the door, turning him for a brief moment into a perfect snowman. Ritchie was pelting towards the village green by the time he heard the man angrily roaring again.

"I'm the district nurse."

CHAPTER 4

As Ritchie got home, a smart red car drew up opposite their house. A lady got out of it, dressed in a smart blue wool coat and a smart little blue hat with a gold badge on it. It looked like some kind of uniform. When she saw Ritchie opening the front gate to go in she said, "Do you live here? Is this Mrs Jacks' house?" Ritchie had to think a moment before he remembered that Mrs Jacks was his mum, and nodded.

"I'm the district nurse," the smart lady said. She had a black case under her arm.

"The door's round here," said Ritchie, pointing round the side of the house, where the back door was.

"Well, I said I'd go in by the front door, and your father was going to leave it open for me," the smart lady replied, "so we'd better just do that."

Ritchie stood on the lawn and watched the district nurse go down the steps to the front door, ring the bell and walk in, calling, "Coo-ee! It's Nurse Howlen! I'll just come up, shall I?"

He went in by the usual door, dumped his schoolbag and then went into the hall. Maisie was already there, listening with her mouth open and her coat trailing from her hand.

"She said she was howling," Maisie whispered, then put her fingers to her lips to show Ritchie should be quiet.

Ritchie couldn't hear much to begin with, but then there were footsteps and the voice of the district nurse ringing down the stairs. "Well, shall we just pop you over on your side while we smooth down the sheet?"

"She's said 'pop' three times already, Maisie remarked, "and she says 'we'll do it' when she just means 'I'll do it'."

Maisie drew herself up very straight and put on a smart-lady expression. "Well, we'll just pop our coat up onto the peg," she said, "and then we'll pop into the kitchen and get some bread and butter. We'll spread a slice for you too, shall we?"

They could hardly eat their bread for giggling, and by the time they had finished it they had decided to call the district nurse Nurse We-We. When she put her head round the door and told them, "We'll just pop off now and catch the chemist," they very nearly choked.

Ritchie went up to Mum's room with

Maisie and for once Mum seemed to be in a good mood and happy to see them home. She was lying propped up on the pillows, and that was unusual. When Maisie told her she thought Nurse Howlen was a very strange lady Mum said, "Oh, but she's so nice – and I want you to be polite to her. She doesn't have any children of her own and she thinks all young people are vandals."

"What's a vandal?" Ritchie asked.

"Oh, someone who damages other people's things," Mum said.

"Like – in their garden, you mean?" said Ritchie anxiously.

"Anywhere, really. Gardens, yes – quite often."

Ritchie said nothing. He went out a few minutes later when Maisie got going on some rigmarole about her school lunch box and how it kept getting swapped round with someone else's who just happened to always have tuna-and-mayonnaise sandwiches which Maisie loved but which Dad never made.

The name felt heavy, like a rock tied round his neck: vandal. Vandal.

That evening, the thaw began. It lasted about a week and was quite unpleasant because the melting snow ran over the hard-packed snow and made it all so slippery it was impossible to walk on. There was wind, and rain, and the stream rose and rose and eventually overflowed its banks and half the people in the village were flooded out. The Jacks' house only had a small flood, not from the stream but because the level of the lawn at the front was quite high, and the melting snow came down the steps to the front door in a waterfall and so into the house. Ritchie often stopped to have a squelch on the soaked patch of carpet by the front door.

Nurse Howlen appeared several times, but though her visits seemed to do Mum some good, they were certainly not good for Dad. He got it into his head that the district nurse wouldn't approve of the state the house was in – although in fact she never paid any attention to that sort of thing – and he would spend the evenings running around putting things away and tidying up, and he seemed to be doing the dusting and hoovering deep into the night. It meant his temper got steadily worse, and he started burning the toast again in the mornings.

So things went on until the Thursday which ever after they spoke of as the Day of the Rice.

The Day of the Rice started badly, and it went on as it started. They were quite late for school, and Dad had forgotten to iron Maisie's school shirt until the last moment, so there was a yellowish, iron-shaped mark on the back of it. What was more, Dad had not been able to capture Can't-Wait to put him outside, which meant the cat would either annoy Mum or leave a mess in the corner, or both.

The evening was worse than the morning. Maisie found that Can't-Wait had made a mess, and she made Ritchie clean it up. When Nurse Howlen came in she told Maisie and Ritchie that they ought to help their father more. When Dad got in he looked worn-out, the colour of a wrung-out dishcloth. He flopped into a chair. "I hate kids," he said. "And I hate teachers and I hate heads of department and I hate janitors and I hate head teachers."

"Why?" Maisie asked, and he told them. It

seemed that he had been so late for school that his class, which was a fourth-form geography class and inclined to be rowdy, had started to riot and overturn the desks. The janitor had found them at it and told another teacher. The other teacher had told the head of department. The head of department had gone to the head teacher and the two heads had called him into the school office and asked him if work was getting too much for him and would he like to see a doctor and get some time off? Dad had been so angry that he had gone back into his class, snarling like a mad dog, and had told the main rowdy boys that if they ever did such a thing again he would punch their lights out.

"What are their lights?" asked Ritchie, enthralled by the tale.

"I don't know," said Dad. "But it really

hurts if you punch them out."

Dad recovered a bit and cooked rice for supper, and made a curry to go with it. Maisie and Ritchie both liked rice – so they wouldn't have complained even if they hadn't both been thinking of Dad snarling like a mad dog. But Dad found rice difficult to eat, or at any rate he found it difficult if he was trying to speak at the same time. He always told Maisie and Ritchie they shouldn't try to eat and talk at the same time, but of course it was different for him.

Maisie had gone through to the kitchen to make up some juice. Dad had just taken a mouthful of rice when Maisie called through, "Which jug should I use?"

"Mm-mm-mm," Dad called back.

"What?"

"For goodness' sake," Dad muttered, and three grains of rice appeared from his mouth, rolled over his lip and fell onto his chin. "Mm-mm-mm," he called louder.

"Which one?" Maisie called, in her most insistent voice.

Dad got up with a growl of irritation and stomped through to the kitchen. Ritchie seized his opportunity and quickly put his plate down on the floor where Can't-Wait was sitting watching him. Ritchie liked rice but was less keen on curry, while Can't-Wait was very keen on curry but didn't care for rice. Can't-Wait's small pink tongue lapped ecstatically.

Ritchie was so busy watching Can't-Wait he didn't notice Dad coming back into the room.

Dad couldn't see the plate on the floor from where he was standing, but he could see well enough that it wasn't on the table. "Bitchie!" he roared, trying at the same time to keep the rice in his mouth, "pot are you pooing?"

Ritchie snatched up the plate, lost his balance and fell off his chair, at the same time catapulting curry and rice across the floor. Can't-Wait ran for cover, but dived back when he noticed a piece of curried something rolling down the wall. Ritchie got up slowly, looking in some horror at the curry dripping from his hand like mud from a swamp. He didn't hear the next thing that Dad roared, because the words were completely muffled by the explosion of half-chewed rice from Dad's mouth. He stood abjectly looking at his curried hand while Dad strode across the room towards him, stepped on his plate, slipped, and sat down, *thump,* on the floor.

Dad wasted no time on groaning, though he must have hurt himself. He reached over, grabbed hold of Ritchie, threw him over his knee and gave him a wallop on the bottom. It was so long since he had done such a thing Ritchie had quite forgotten what it felt like. But as he struggled to his feet again he remembered well enough to know he didn't like it one bit and he was so furious he came right back and punched Dad (it happened to be with his curried hand) as hard as he could. He wasn't sure where he had punched him but he hoped it was his lights. Dad grabbed him again, threw him over his knee again, and walloped him twice on the bottom, much harder. "You want to see who can hit hardest?" he thundered. "Try that again and you'll soon see!"

Ritchie rushed from the room, his face burning with rage, tears spouting from his eyes like water from a boiling kettle.

He dimly heard Maisie screaming, "Dad,

you shouldn't have done that – that was bad!" But he took no notice of this unexpected support and shut himself in the bedroom and, after first wiping his hand clean on Maisie's bedcover, piled boxes against the door to stop it being opened by anyone.

"There's Orion," said Dad.

CHAPTER 5

Ritchie listened. Everything seemed very quiet in the house. Soundlessly, he unpiled the boxes that were against the door and very softly opened it. Now he could hear the sound of Maisie sobbing, somewhere upstairs – probably in Mum's room. He peeped round the door of the living-room. It was empty. He peeped into the kitchen. It was empty too. He breathed a sigh of relief. He opened the door at one end of the kitchen that led past the coat pegs to the back door.

He had decided he would put his boots on and go outside. Sometimes he felt he couldn't breathe inside the house. It was as though there was no air, as though something – perhaps like a giant foot – was pressing down on the house, crushing it and squeezing out the air. He knew it was because of Mum always lying up there in bed that he felt this. And tonight he had to get out.

The back door was open and Dad was sitting on the doorstep. Although it was dark Ritchie could see that his shoulders were moving – twitching or shaking in a strange way. Strange for Dad, anyway: not strange for Maisie. Dad was crying. He was crying quite silently, you only knew he was crying because of the way his shoulders were moving. Ritchie didn't know what to do. As quietly as he could, he picked up his boots.

He wasn't quiet enough. Dad heard him

and turned round. Ritchie shut his eyes, waiting for the yell. But Dad didn't yell. He just said, in a nearly normal voice – though it sounded as though his nose was a bit stuffed up – "You've decided to go out too, have you? I was going to go out but I didn't get any farther than the door."

Ritchie didn't say anything. Dad pulled out a handkerchief, made a sound in it like a trumpeting elephant, and then patted his knee. "Come here," he said. Ritchie went to him, a little warily. Dad put his arm round him. With Dad sitting down, their faces were on a level. "Listen," said Dad. "That was bad, what you did. I think you know that."

Ritchie nodded gravely.

"But it wasn't that bad," Dad went on. "In fact, it was just silly, it wasn't even bad at all. And Maisie's right, I shouldn't have smacked you: that was bad. It's just all getting too much for me, you see. Everything – school, and this housekeeping, and looking after you two. I'm not much good at it, you see... And worrying about Mum. That's the worst thing really, the worrying. Anyway – I promise, I won't ever smack you like that again, not ever."

Ritchie glanced at him, uncertainly, then looked outside. In the darkness he could see the outline of the hill against the dim light of stars.

"Do you want to go for a walk?" Dad said. "It's getting on for your bedtime but – well, what does it matter? What does anything matter?"

Ritchie nodded, and started to put his boots on. He got the first one on, then paused. "Is Mum going to die?" he asked.

Dad took a deep breath. "I don't know,"

he said finally. "She could, I suppose. I hope she doesn't."

Ritchie thought about this. He wasn't sure what he really felt, but the first thought that came to him was that if Mum died at least they wouldn't have her lying up there in bed, pressing down on the house, making it so difficult to breathe. As soon as he had thought this he felt terrified that she might die because he had thought it. He dropped his other boot and clung onto Dad, burying his head against him.

"Come on," Dad whispered at last. "It might not come to that. Sometimes I think it will, sometimes I think it won't. Tonight, I think it won't. In fact, tonight, for some reason, I feel everything's going to be all right. Let's go for a walk."

They took the road out of the village, up towards the hill. As they left the village lights behind them, the stars grew brighter. The wind was very cold, but Ritchie was well wrapped up.

"There's Orion," said Dad, pointing back downhill to a big shape of stars stretched like a ghost over the village. Ritchie felt strangely comforted. Orion was like a giant ghost, and he had not seen ghosts for such a long time. Once, he remembered, he had seen them everywhere: he had not been sure then if he was scared of them or if he liked them, but now he was quite certain that he liked them. Giants too. Orion was a giant ghost.

They reached the top of the road, climbed a fence and set off across a dark stubble-field. Ritchie felt the stubble swishing against his boots like the bristles of a giant hairbrush.

"We'd better not go up the hill," Dad said. "We really would be late then. We'll go along the foot of it and then back down." He stopped. "Look!" he exclaimed suddenly.

Over the whole northern horizon there was something like a faint silver-and-pale-lilac rainbow. It was too flat to be a proper rainbow, as well as having no proper colours, but it was very distinct.

"That," said Dad, "must be the Northern Lights. If we lived farther north it would be brighter and higher. It probably means bad weather's coming."

"Will we have more snow?" asked Ritchie.

"Probably," Dad answered.

"Perhaps it'll be a white Christmas," said Ritchie.

The Day of the Rice had started badly, and had gone on badly: but it didn't finish badly. It finished well, but it also finished with the strangest thing they had ever seen.

When they got back to the garden gate,

they saw Maisie across the lawn, standing by the corner of the house. At first they thought she was worried about them, but it turned out it wasn't that at all.

"There's something making a funny noise," she said, pointing over in the direction of the hill. Its outline was black and sharp, but it seemed that it wasn't the starlight now but the pale light in the north that was making it stand out so clear.

"We didn't hear anything funny," Dad said. "And we were up there."

"Listen," said Maisie.

It was like a faint humming, very low down, very deep and soft: *Hum-de-ree-de-ra-de-ree, hum-de-ree-de-ra-de-ree,* with a rhythm that changed slightly, now quickening, now slowing down. And the ground – as they noticed now but had not noticed before – the ground was shaking very slightly. Ritchie knew that shaking, and his heart began to beat faster.

"Look," said Maisie, pointing up towards the outline of the hill.

The hill had changed. A part of the side of it seemed to be bulging out, bulging upwards. Not a very large bulge: a bulge like a black moon rising. And just when this black moon seemed to have risen clear of the side of the hill, something square rose after it: square, but with rounded corners, and then the square thing moved and became something more like the outline of a tree with two raised branches. But more and more of the shadowy thing was rising against the eerie northern light, rising taller and taller into the sky, and all the time the faint humming, and the slight shaking of the ground, went on.

And now the shadow had stopped rising.

It was complete: a human shadow, the black outline of a huge human shape, which raised its arms high as if stretching up to the stars, then lowered them and began moving its hands about, the way you do if you've been lying on them and they've got pins and needles. And then the legs moved, the knees raising, one after the other, and the huge figure seemed to be taking short steps up and down the side of the hill, raising its knees slightly more than it would need to for ordinary steps. The humming grew a little louder, and its rhythm was almost like a dance step: *Hum-um-de-ree-de-ra-de-ree-dum, hum-um-de-ree-de-ra-de-ree-dum.*

Sometimes the figure was side-on, sometimes facing towards (or away from) them. Then it seemed to bend down slightly and straighten up again; bend and straighten, bend and straighten. It was

*The huge figure seemed to be taking short steps
up and down the side of the hill.*

holding the palms of its hands flat, one out in front, one out behind; the knees going up and down, the back bending and straightening, the jigging rhythm of the hum...

"It's doing a boogie," breathed Dad. "It's boogieing on the hill."

"It's a giant," whispered Ritchie.

"Not much doubt about that," Dad agreed. "At least four times the height of a tree."

"Will it eat us?" squeaked Maisie, for once in her life impressed.

"Doesn't look like it," said Dad. "I can't help thinking it looks remarkably good-tempered."

"It's hopping," said Ritchie. "Look, it's hopping up the hill."

Indeed it was. They watched the great shape take several hops to the top of the hill.

Four hops, and four huge soft *bumps* reverberated round the countryside. The roof of the house rattled quietly. The figure was standing on top of the hill, standing on one foot with the other raised and held out.

"Watch out!" Dad yelled, and sweeping Maisie and Ritchie together off their feet, he hurled them forwards on their faces into a flower-bed. A split second later two slates rattled over the edge of the roof and crashed onto the path where they had been standing.

"Must have been shaken loose," Dad muttered, scrambling to his knees. "Better get that roof checked."

When they looked again, the figure on the hilltop was gone.

Ritchie went off by himself.

CHAPTER 6

The Day of the Rice had been a Thursday. It was quite clear all through Friday that it was going to snow again. The breeze was bitterly cold, and grey cloud like wrinkled wool built up gradually – or rather, built down, because every new layer of cloud was lower than the one before. It was almost dark when they got out of school, but the snow had not yet begun to fall.

Ritchie told Maisie the same story he had told her before, then went off by himself, waited at the bridge, and wandered down to the green. Here he walked up and down on the squashy matted grass, thinking hard.

He wasn't sure what he was going to do, but he knew he had to do something. He knew beyond a shadow of doubt that in some mysterious way the stone boot and the gigantic shape on the hillside were connected. That first time, when he had put his arm into the stone boot, he had seemed to see a giant's feet, one bare, one with a boot on. The next time, when he had dropped the boot, there had been that shaking of the earth. And before that, he remembered, there had been the landslip on the hill – back in that dry weather in springtime, when the water in the stream had been low. The landslip must have happened when the stone boot was being stolen from the stream.

And now he realized what the giant had been doing the night before. At the end of its dance it had been hopping on its booted foot and then it had held its other foot up, as if to show anyone who was watching that it was missing its other boot.

Ritchie wandered along beside the stream as it ambled round the edge of the green. At last he pushed his way through the thin part of the hedge. He at once came upon a low fence. It didn't even come up to his knee. He could see, now that there was no snow, that the snow path he had followed to the garden of statues led through a series of gardens, each marked by a low fence like the first. He quite definitely had no right to be here, and after last time he might get into serious trouble if he was seen here again.

Then it occurred to him that even if he did manage to take the stone boot away, he wouldn't know what to do with it. If he dropped it back in the stream someone would just find it again. If he took it home with him it would definitely look like stealing.

Ritchie's feet decided what he had to do almost without him having to think about it. They led him down the bank and into the shallow water of the stream. At least, it was shallow at other times, when the level was normal. Now, after the melting of the snow, it came up to his knees, and his trousers clung heavily to his legs. The water was bitterly cold. After a few steps his feet stopped squelching in his shoes and he couldn't tell whether his legs were freezing or burning. He waded on down the stream. All he could see of the houses over the bank was the tops of their roofs, but he counted the chimney stacks to work out how far along he was going. There must have been about six gardens before he came to the garden of statues, so that meant he would have to count twelve chimney stacks.

Ten – eleven – twelve. He stood for a moment in the water, trying to keep his balance against the current. The darkness was about right: dark enough so that no one would see him, but not so dark that he couldn't see.

The stone boot hadn't been put back up the ladder, but it had been set upright at the base of it. Ritchie slodged heavily over to it. His legs felt very uncomfortable, so heavy with water, and so cold, he could hardly move them. He moved his schoolbag properly onto his back and looked down at the boot. What was he to do? He knew it was too heavy to lift, and he couldn't drag it all the way home.

He lifted his foot up and held it over the opening of the boot. The rims of his shoe would get stuck on the sides if he tried to put it on – but if he took the shoe off, he thought he might just fit his foot in. It seemed a stupid thing to do, as he had no hope of walking in a boot that was too heavy to lift – but he was curious to do it, all the same.

He tugged the wet shoe off and put it carefully in his schoolbag, which he zipped up. Then he unzipped it again and took the sock off too and plopped it in. Then he pulled his soaking trouser leg up to the knee, and carefully eased his bare foot and bare leg into the stone boot.

It felt rough on his cold-tender skin, and to begin with very unpleasant, and he was just about to pull his foot out again when he realized that it no longer felt cold. In fact, it felt quite snug. He wriggled his toes farther down, touched the bottom, pushed his foot in flat. The boot was on.

He stood, and smiled. He knew he had a

soaking cold leg and he ought to do something about it. But the rest of him felt so snug and warm – as if the whole of the rest of him was actually inside a warm boot. He smiled, and looked around at the dim blue world.

The world seemed to have grown bigger – or perhaps it was smaller? He could see his own house at the other end of the village: he could get there in a couple of steps, if he wanted to – that was how near it seemed... But perhaps he would have a sleep first. After all, he thought, he had taken thousands of years to get to where he was now. He could afford to sleep for a couple of hundred more.

Just then his leg – the cold leg – collapsed, and he came down heavily onto his knee. That brought him round suddenly, and he blinked several times. That was all nonsense, about taking thousands of years to get here! How could he have thought that? He had got here from school, that same afternoon! And here he was, in a garden he shouldn't be in, in a stone boot that didn't belong to him, at the wrong end of the village!

He forced the booted leg straight and with a great effort managed to stand. The other leg – the cold leg – immediately threatened to give way again. He would have to take the boot off and get home, even if it meant crawling. He teetered, and then, without thinking, took a step to get his balance back.

Took a step with the stone boot.

He had been able to move it, with perfect ease! He took another step. His foot felt as light and springy as if he were wearing soft-soled trainers. He stretched his toes and bounced on the foot, then took a huge hop – halfway across the garden. It was

Ritchie hopped over the low fence.

unbelievable! He hopped again, out of the garden of statues, over the low fence, into the neighbouring garden – the snowman's garden – then bounce-bounce-bounce across it, and over the next fence. It was wonderful.

His other leg had started to come back to life a little, and was just managing to support him between each hop – otherwise he wouldn't have been able to keep his balance and would have fallen over – but it felt so weak and wobbly it made him want to giggle. Each time he used it to support him he lurched over towards the ground before the booted leg took the strain. He suddenly wondered if this was what it felt like for Can't-Wait, always having to run along with one of his front legs missing.

Ritchie burst through the hedge onto the village green, crossed it in seven hops and bounced all the way back up the main street of the village. There was no one about, or at any rate no one that he noticed.

When he got back home there seemed to be a lot of cars outside the house. One of them was Dad's and it occurred to him that it must be later than he had thought. He was going to be in trouble, but the journey home had been so delightful that it was worth a bit of trouble. Besides, he had the stone boot at last. He had stolen it. He was a thief. He didn't care.

He slipped it off and wiggled it along the ground under a bush out of sight at the side of the garage. Then he took a deep breath and went in.

He was not very late. It seemed that Mum had got suddenly worse and had rung Dad's school and Dad had come home early and then called for the doctor. The doctor was

Ritchie bounced all the way back up the main street.

here now and so was Nurse Howlen, and there was a lot of bustle and hushed voices. Maisie loudly demanded to know why Ritchie was going about with one bare foot, then marched off to get some clean trousers for him. No one paid any attention to them. Ritchie took his school trousers off and put them in the washing basket and wished he was outside, bouncing in the stone boot, a thousand miles away from nurses and doctors and bossy sisters and sick mothers.

The nurse and the doctor left, and Dad came downstairs, slowly, gripping the bannister and looking like an old man. He stood in the kitchen for a while, looking hopelessly around at the dirty dishes and the vegetables in the vegetable rack and then said they would go down to the fish and chip shop. When they got out to the car the snow had started.

Dad liked the hopping as much as Ritchie had.

CHAPTER 7

It snowed, off and on, for most of Saturday. Maisie and Ritchie went out a couple of times and dodged among the large, wide-spaced snowflakes falling through the muffled grey air. Ritchie didn't mention the stone boot to Maisie. He was feeling a bit worried again about stealing, and he tried for a long time to pretend that the boot wasn't there in its hiding-place beside the garage. In the end he had to go and check – and of course then he wanted to try it on again. But he couldn't get rid of Maisie, who for some reason seemed to want to be his one-and-only companion this weekend. He didn't want to tell her about the boot yet, so he waited, and worried.

Mum didn't seem any worse – at any rate, it didn't seem as though she was going to die on the spot – and Dad was busy with housework for most of the day. The whole house was festooned with washing which he hadn't been able to hang outside, and he dodged in and out among it, bent doggedly over the Hoover. It seemed the district nurse was going to be coming even more often, and she would "pop in" on Sunday morning. Maisie had got bored with calling her Nurse We-We, and if Ritchie did, she looked down her nose at him and told him Nurse Howlen was doing Mum a lot of good.

"Why's she getting worse then?" asked Ritchie.

"Shut up," said Maisie. "You don't know anything."

The snow was nothing like as deep as last time, and Sunday came up sparkling and bright.

"Dad!" Maisie called. "Can't-Wait's doing the toilet right in the middle of the path!"

Dad threw the window open and bellowed, "What's wrong with under the hedge, same as every other time?"

Can't-Wait, who by this time was carefully sniffing the little dark pile on the white ground, glanced up at them coolly and started to scrape the snow over it.

When Nurse Howlen arrived she began as usual, but Ritchie heard her stop in the middle of cheerily asking Mum how she was and say, in quite a different voice, "Oh, I've stepped in something. What an awful smell."

She came down the stairs a little while later carrying the offending shoe which Dad insisted on taking from her and cleaning outside the back door. Nurse Howlen stood on one foot in the kitchen and asked Dad if he was still managing with his teaching.

Dad just replied, "I hate kids," which set Nurse Howlen off talking about how children nowadays weren't brought up properly and how parents didn't set any standards and how most of them were little better than ruffians.

"Vandals," she said. "They destroy things, just for the fun of it. And stealing – just wait till you hear this. My husband and I, well, we collect garden ornaments. You know, it's our little hobby, and our garden isn't near any footpath or anywhere where people go – it's quite secluded, at the back of a row of houses – and do you know they come along from the village green through all our neighbours' gardens just to get in and pick on ours. Statues and ornaments, you know, that's the sort of thing we collect, it's just our hobby. And Mr White next door, he saw one of them come in – that last fall of snow it was – bold as brass, right into the middle of the garden and start knocking the things about. And would you believe it, they went off with something on Friday night – just whipped it clean out of the garden."

"Oh, I'd believe it," Dad growled. "I'd believe anything of them."

"We're just going to have to put up a proper big fence," Nurse Howlen said. "It's the only thing for it – and it's such a shame, because all our neighbours so enjoy looking at our little collection, but what can you do..."

Dad presented her with her shoe, cleaned, and apologized again. "Not much you can do about cats," he said. "They've a mind of their own."

Ritchie could hardly believe his bad luck. Of course it would be her garden, of all people's! What was he to do now? He couldn't think of any safe hiding-place, and Nurse Howlen was sure to peer round the side of the garage one of these days and recognize the stone boot. What would he do if she did? He could pretend he didn't know how it had got there. But then what if the snowman, that Mr White, got to hear about it and recognized him?

Dad noticed Ritchie looking worried and asked him what the matter was. At any other time Ritchie might have not told him. But the Day of the Rice was still fresh in his mind, and the extraordinary thing they had seen together on the hill. Ritchie felt he could trust Dad. He took him round to the garage and pointed.

"It was me in the nurse's garden," he said. "I took that."

Dad stared in disbelief, first at the boot, then at Ritchie, then back at the boot.

When the silence had gone on long enough Ritchie said, "You said you wouldn't smack me again." As soon as he had said it he wished he hadn't: that was just the sort of comment that could send Dad into a roaring rage.

But when Dad eventually spoke, what he said had nothing to do with thievery or vandalism. "How on earth did you get it home?" he asked wonderingly. "It must weigh sixty or seventy pounds. You're not that strong."

Ritchie screwed up his face. "I wore it," he said. "Honestly, it wasn't theirs," he went on. "I found it first, in the stream. They dragged it out and put it in their garden..."

"You wore it?"

"I – I put it on. And then I bounced. It wasn't heavy." Ritchie scratched his head. His story did seem very unlikely, even to him.

Dad reached in and heaved the stone boot out of its hiding-place. "Sixty pounds at the very least," he gasped. He bent down and inspected it. "Look how detailed it is. Look at that stitching – I've never seen such fine chisel work. From a distance it looks just like a real boot."

"It's that giant's boot," Ritchie said.

Dad didn't immediately tell him not to be silly. He looked very thoughtful. Suddenly he lifted his own foot up – he was wearing his slippers – and fitted it over the top of the hole. It was just what Ritchie had done, two days before.

"I had to take my shoe and sock off," Ritchie said. "And it just fitted. It doesn't feel like stone inside."

Dad went on staring at the boot and, almost as though his mind was on something completely different, pulled off his slipper and sock and dropped them onto the snow. Then he pushed his foot, with very little effort, down inside the boot. It fitted him.

He smiled. "You're right," he murmured. "How right you are. How very snug it is. It's like being tucked up in bed. Oh" – he yawned – "I think I could just catch up on some sleep..." He closed his eyes, still smiling.

"Dad!" Ritchie shouted. "Don't fall asleep. It – there's something funny about it, it..."

Dad blinked, still smiling. "What was that?"

"It's better to hop in it," Ritchie said. "It's more fun."

"Hop, eh?" said Dad. "All right." And he hopped.

It was soon obvious that he liked the hopping as much as Ritchie had. With Dad it was more of a proper hop-and-a-skip because his other leg wasn't half-dead with cold as Ritchie's had been. He hopped around the garden, whooping with delight, for fully half an hour. Maisie came out and started running round the garden after him, screaming with laughter and yelling at him to stop, and Ritchie ran after them both, yelling anything that came into his head. Can't-Wait appeared as well and hopped and capered and shot up and down trees.

Surprisingly, Maisie didn't demand to

have a turn with the stone boot, even though Ritchie then told her he had hopped in it as well as Dad. "So you found it at last, did you?" she said, with a grin of pure glee. "It's about time too."

And surprisingly, Ritchie didn't want to have another turn with it now either. It was as though both of them felt in some way that it was Dad's boot, for today at any rate. And the sun and the sparkling snow and the blue sky made them feel as though they hadn't seen sun, or brightness, for months.

They could laugh and shout, as loud as they liked. And until Dad took the boot off, that was what they did.

Ritchie felt himself lifted into the air.

CHAPTER 8

For five days after that – the last full week of the school term – Dad hardly spoke at all. He just smiled. Ritchie knew what that smile meant. It meant that Dad was half-thinking that perhaps it was true he had taken thousands of years to get to where he was now; and if he felt like it he really could just put the boot on and snuggle into it and sleep for a hundred years or so. It wouldn't make that much difference.

He didn't take the washing down. Other people were putting up their Christmas decorations. Maisie and Ritchie's house was decorated with streamers of sheets and garlands of towels and wreaths of underpants.

They were late for school every single day. Dad still got the breakfast, and their packed lunches, but he didn't hurry over anything. He never burned the toast. He just smiled, and did everything very slowly, and sometimes simply stood for minutes on end, gazing at nothing in particular. When Maisie and Ritchie realized that they weren't going to be harried and hassled, they slowed down as well. Maisie took quarter of an hour to put on her tights, and Ritchie turned his vest over twenty times, very carefully, just to make sure he didn't get it on back to front. His cuff buttons didn't get done up once that week. One morning they were so late that Dad's school rang him up to see why he hadn't arrived. "I'm just on my way," he said calmly. "No need to get so worked up."

"This isn't good enough, you know," Maisie's teacher told her sourly, when for the third time she walked in halfway through the first class. "Things are going to have to improve."

Maisie told Ritchie about this on the way back from school, and they agreed that as it was important to keep Dad smiling, but also important to get to school on time, they would have to get up earlier and get their own breakfast. They did, and it worked very well. On the fifth morning Maisie even managed to get their packed lunches ready, before Dad had come into the kitchen.

Not once during those five days was Ritchie even tempted to put on the boot himself. He knew he would have another turn, eventually. On Friday night, there was a feeling in his throat like a lump that wanted to come up into his mouth. He realized he was feeling sad – desperately sad – sad enough to cry. Perhaps it was because it was the end of the week, he thought, and it had been such a lovely week. But just before he fell asleep he understood that it was because the stone boot wasn't his, or Dad's, and he was going to have to take it back to where it came from.

It was the first thing he thought of when he woke the next morning, but now the terrible sadness seemed to have gone. He waited all day. None of them talked about the boot. He waited until after supper, when he saw the moon coming up. Dad was with Mum in her bedroom. "Tell Dad I'm taking the stone boot back," he told Maisie.

"To Nurse Howlen?" Maisie asked. "Are you going to tell her?"

Ritchie just smiled. He took a carrier bag and dropped one wellington and one sock into it, put on the other wellington, and hopped outside with one bare foot.

The days that week had been mild and sunny, and the nights had been frosty, so a lot of the snow had gone, but great streaks of it still lay across the fields and glimmered in the moonlight. The sky on the southern horizon was pale, violet. Ritchie turned his back to it, and started to hop, in the stone boot, strongly and joyously, over the fields up towards the hill. The boot crunched through the frosty crust down onto snow and mud, yet he felt as light as thistledown. *Crunch-crunch-crunch*, the ground sped back behind him.

He had not thought where he was going on the hill, but as he went on it seemed obvious that he should make for the point halfway up its right-hand side, where the giant's head had first appeared. The hill lay calm and milky in the light of the oval moon. He climbed without effort, and looked down the slope at the far side where the snow-covered ground lay twisted into ditches and towers, silver and black-shadowed: the place of the landslip. There was no eerie light tonight on the northern sky. The only light was the soft moonlight, and the stars were dim.

He stopped, sat down, and tugged off the boot. He reached in the bag and fished out his sock and wellington, and put them on. The stone boot stood in front of him, hard and cold. He pushed it over the edge of the rock face, down into the shadowed snow below, and it disappeared.

Nothing happened, and Ritchie began to feel cold. He scrambled to his feet, peered down into the landslip once more, and started off for home. It was all downhill, and the ground wasn't rough, but it felt such hard going after the glorious skipping of the boot. The lights of the village stretched, dull orange, in front of him – but they seemed so far away. Ritchie felt he was never going to manage it home.

Then: *Hum-de-ree-de-ra-de-ree-da, hum-um-de-ree-de-ra-de-ree-dara*. It was loud this time, but not deafening, and beautifully musical. The ground wasn't exactly shaking: he felt as though he were walking over the surface of a drum, which was echoing and resonating to his step.

Hum-de-ree-de-ra-de-ree-da, hum-de-ree-de-ra-de-ree-da. Ritchie didn't stop, or look round, and he didn't feel scared, and he was not in the least surprised when something took him gently round the waist and he felt himself lifted, ever so gently, into the air, higher and higher – higher than a treetop, much higher, four times as high.

He was sitting on something that felt like a close-woven net of ropes. He gripped onto it at either side of him, to steady himself, not out of fright, but because he was tipping gently backwards and forwards in time with the *ree-da* of the huge, yet peaceful, humming. He was on the giant's shoulder. The great cloud-like head beside him was turned half-on to the moon so that he was in its shadow, and he couldn't tell what the face looked like. The village lights came closer at tremendous speed.

Some distance before the village, they stopped, and Ritchie was set gently – ever so gently – back down on the ground. He walked on a little way, then, hearing the humming suddenly stop, and a large noise like a rustling of trees and a creaking of branches, he turned round and saw that the

The village lights came closer at tremendous speed.

giant had settled itself on the ground.

It was even bigger than he had expected, and it was smiling. It was sitting in the field humped like a cornstack with its rounded belly resting snugly on its crossed legs. It had no beard – in fact, it had no hair at all. And Ritchie could see by the great eyes that glimmered like pearls in the moonlight that it was blind.

"Good night," he said.

The giant smiled on.

Ritchie walked slowly backwards, until he bumped into Dad at the edge of the field. Maisie was with him, looking as though she might start gibbering at any moment.

"Are you all right?" Dad said anxiously, then, seeing that Ritchie was smiling, "You rascal! We've been all the way over to Nurse Howlen's house. You knew we'd do that, didn't you?"

The giant was even bigger than Ritchie had expected.

"I didn't tell a lie," Ritchie said quickly. "I said I was taking the boot back. Does that nurse know I took it?"

"We just said you'd found it," Dad said, "and you'd been going to take it back. That was true enough. *Now* we'll have some explaining to do."

"What is that?" Maisie asked, gaping up the field at the great dark hump with the faint, misty-gleaming eyes.

"The giant," said Ritchie. "It's got two boots now."

"I want to go home," said Maisie.

They woke late the next morning. Ritchie was the first up. He went out the back door and squinted in the golden light of the newly risen sun. There was a lovely smell coming from somewhere. Over by the garage, the bush behind which he had hidden the stone boot had burst into small purple blossoms. That was where the scent was coming from.

Shielding his eyes from the light, Ritchie tried to make out what the dark shape was he saw darting here and there on the lawn at the front. Yes, it was a cat. It was Can't-Wait rushing around like a kitten, doing salmon-leaps into the air and trying to catch small midges between his paws.

Between his paws. No, surely, Ritchie thought – it can't be Can't-Wait after all. This dancing lunatic of a cat had four paws.

But it was Can't-Wait.

And next moment Ritchie was rushing back into the house, blundering into the dark hallway to shout out to everyone to come and see the amazing thing that had happened –

But he forgot to, because Mum was coming down the stairs towards him, her hand moving lightly along the washing-draped bannister.

She was in her dressing-gown, and she looked rather pale and wobbly, and her hair looked lank and greasy still, but she had brushed it and it fell straight and neat around her shoulders. And she was smiling. Ritchie couldn't remember when he had last seen Mum smile. He meant to run up to meet her, and tell her he was sorry for all the bad things he had been thinking about her, but he sat down sharply on the floor instead. And Mum got to the bottom of the stairs, and bent down and she was strong enough to pick him up and hold him in her arms.

Ritchie clung on with his arms round her neck. And it flashed through his mind then that he had never once thought that the giant could be bad or bloodthirsty – and that was strange, because it was not what the stories

Mum was strong enough to pick Ritchie up and hold him.

said about giants. This giant, anyway, was a bringer of gifts: gifts so wonderful it made you almost ashamed to have them. He breathed, slowly, deeply. Mum was a bit smelly: she had been in bed for too long. But there was the old, familiar Mum-smell, too – the right smell. She was all right. Whatever he had thought about her when she was ill, she was all right now.

THE

END